P. I. Tchaikovsky's

# SWAN LAKE

illustrated by Shigeru Hatsuyama
adapted by Eriko Kishida
translated by Ann King Herring

**Fantasia Pictorial**
Stories from Famous Music

Frederick Warne

Long, long ago, in a castle by a lake deep in the forest, there lived a young prince. His name was Siegfried.

One day the old princess, his mother, came to him and said, "Tomorrow, my son, you will be twenty-one. In honour of your birthday, I have planned to hold a grand ball. The most beautiful girls from near and far will come as guests."

She paused and looked thoughtfully at Siegfried for a moment before going on, "And from among them, you must choose the one who will be your bride."

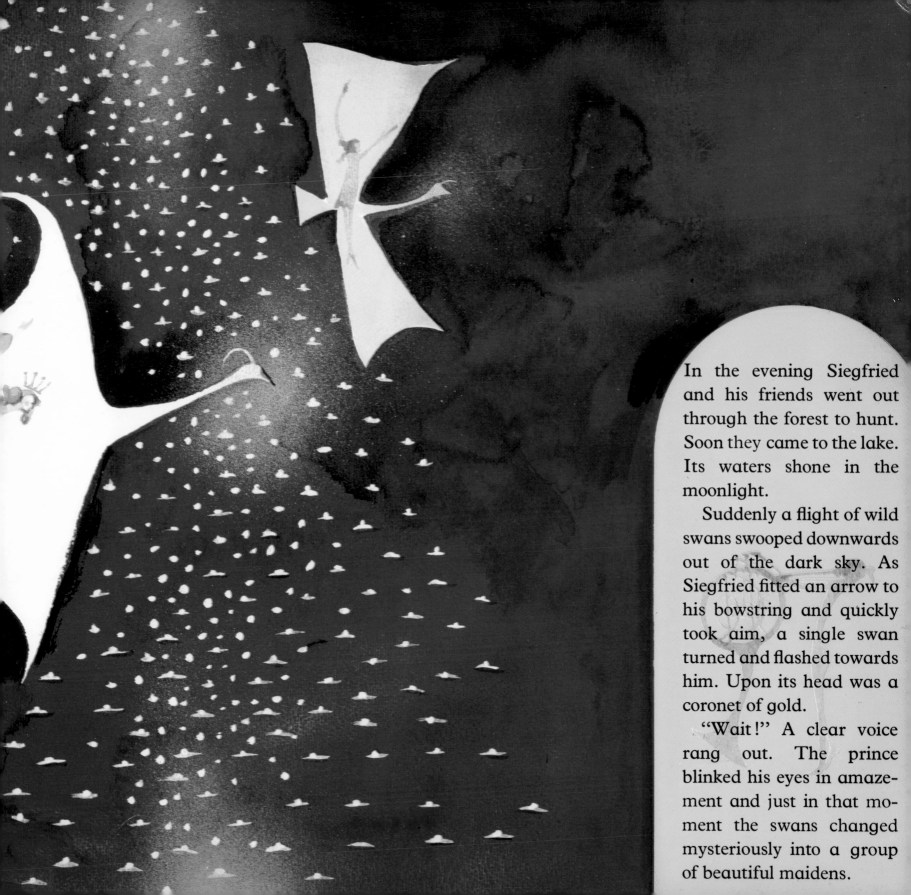

In the evening Siegfried and his friends went out through the forest to hunt. Soon they came to the lake. Its waters shone in the moonlight.

Suddenly a flight of wild swans swooped downwards out of the dark sky. As Siegfried fitted an arrow to his bowstring and quickly took aim, a single swan turned and flashed towards him. Upon its head was a coronet of gold.

"Wait!" A clear voice rang out. The prince blinked his eyes in amazement and just in that moment the swans changed mysteriously into a group of beautiful maidens.

"We are not really swans. We are human beings, just as you are. But an evil magician has cast a spell upon us, so that we can only return to our true form from midnight until dawn," said the girl with the golden crown. "My name is Odette, and I am the queen of the swans."

"When will the spell be broken?" Siegfried asked.

"Whenever and wherever a prince shall ask me to marry him. But he must be true in heart and in deed," she replied.

Siegfried took her hand in his.

"At the ball tomorrow evening I must choose the one who is to be my bride. Now that I have seen you how could I choose any other? Come to the ball, Odette. I shall not fail you."

Gazing happily into one another's eyes, they never saw the dark shape that sat in a tree nearby, watching and listening. It was the magician, disguised as an owl.

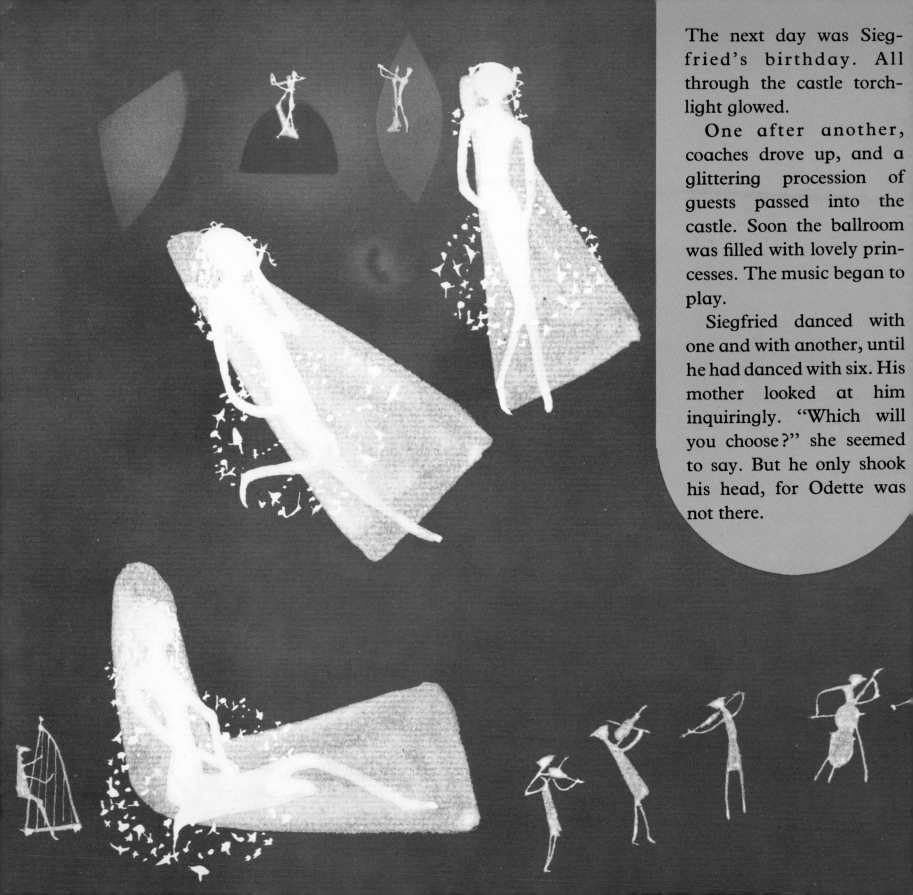

The next day was Siegfried's birthday. All through the castle torchlight glowed.

One after another, coaches drove up, and a glittering procession of guests passed into the castle. Soon the ballroom was filled with lovely princesses. The music began to play.

Siegfried danced with one and with another, until he had danced with six. His mother looked at him inquiringly. "Which will you choose?" she seemed to say. But he only shook his head, for Odette was not there.

At that moment the trumpets sounded. Torches flickered low, and a chill wind blew through the hall as an elderly nobleman entered, leading with him a striking girl in a black gown. Siegfried gasped. "Odette!" he thought. "At last you have come."

Siegfried danced with the girl, and when the dance was ended he took her to his mother's chair and announced to all: "This is the one whom I have chosen."

"Music!" the guests shouted joyfully. "Music for Siegfried and his lady."

Then, from the darkness outside the ballroom windows, there came a rustle, like the beating of swan wings. Another voice spoke out.

"Siegfried! Here I am. That is not Odette at your side. The magician has tricked you, and you have failed me." The girl in black smiled mockingly, as the rustle of swan wings grew fainter and ceased altogether.

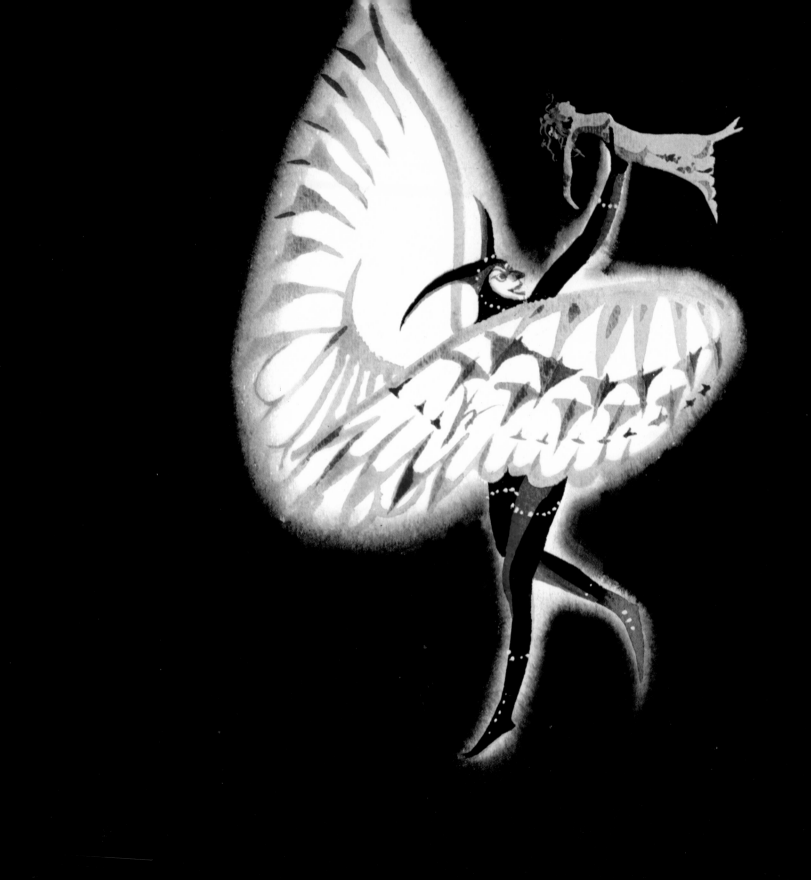

Siegfried turned on the nobleman and demanded angrily, "Who, then, are you?"

Suddenly all the lights went out and an eerie blackness filled the hall. "Ha, ha! Don't you know who I am? And as for your bride-to-be, she is my own daughter, Odile. I have triumphed over you," the magician gloated. "Now you will never set Odette free."

He laughed wickedly and swept out of the room.

Drawing his sword, Siegfried rushed after the magician. "Odette," he cried, "forgive me. I must and will set you free. Die, vile sorcerer!"

The young prince attacked so fiercely that the magician was taken by surprise. But as he fell, mortally wounded, he looked at Siegfried and laughed.

"Foolish Prince, despair! You can kill me, yes, but you can never break the spell." The magician hissed out his last breath.

With new hope, Siegfried ran out into the night.

By the lake shore a faint echo of ringing bells drifted across the water as the swan maidens waited for Odette. They spoke in whispers.

"When she returns surely she will bring the prince with her."

"The two of them will be married soon, and then we shall all be free for ever."

But Odette came back alone. With tears in her voice, she spoke.

"Try to be brave, and not to weep. I was too late. The prince has chosen the magician's daughter. For us there is no hope left."

At that moment Siegfried arrived out of breath.

"Odette!" he pleaded. "Listen to me. I have killed the magician!"

But Odette only wept.

"That is not enough, Siegfried. We are still in his power."

"How is it possible?"

"Because you broke your promise to me. If we prove our love stronger than death, Siegfried, only then will the swan maidens be set free."

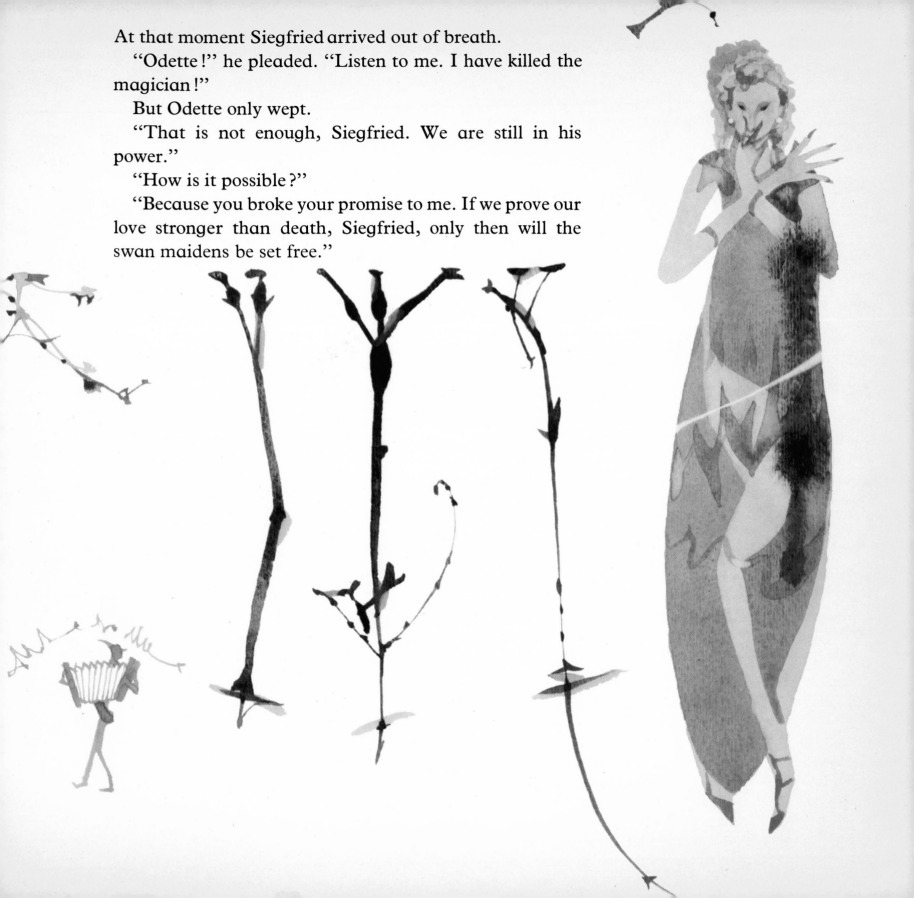

Then she ran towards the lake and threw herself into the water.

"Odette, wait! Wherever you go, I will go with you, for I love no one else but you."

He seized her hand, and together they sank into the depths of the lake.

On the bank the swan maidens knelt, as they watched the dark waters sadly.

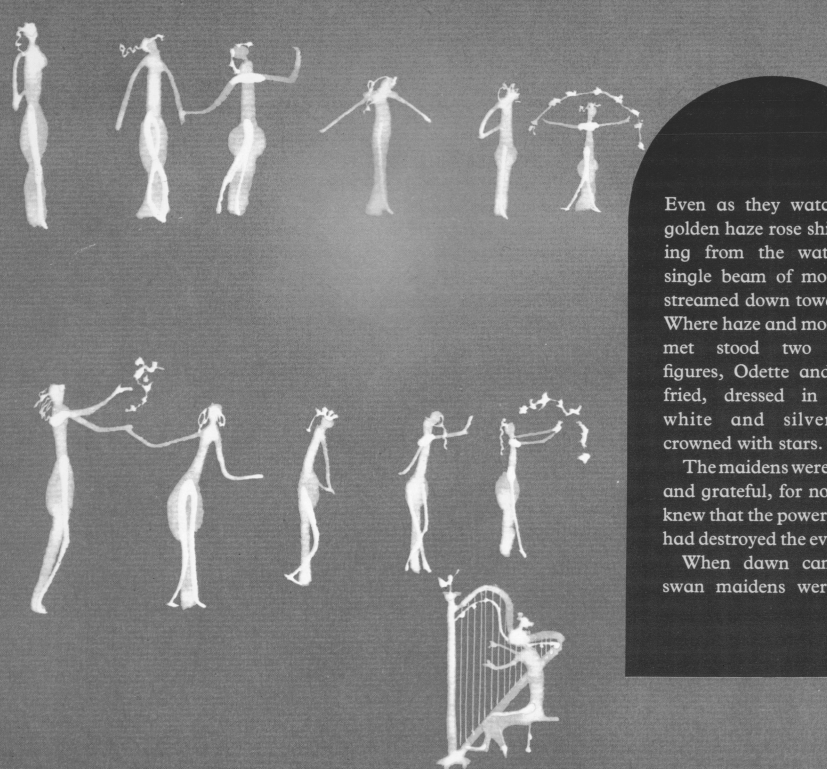

Even as they watched, a golden haze rose shimmering from the waters. A single beam of moonlight streamed down towards it. Where haze and moonlight met stood two bright figures, Odette and Siegfried, dressed in bridal white and silver and crowned with stars.

The maidens were happy and grateful, for now they knew that the power of love had destroyed the evil spell.

When dawn came the swan maidens were free.